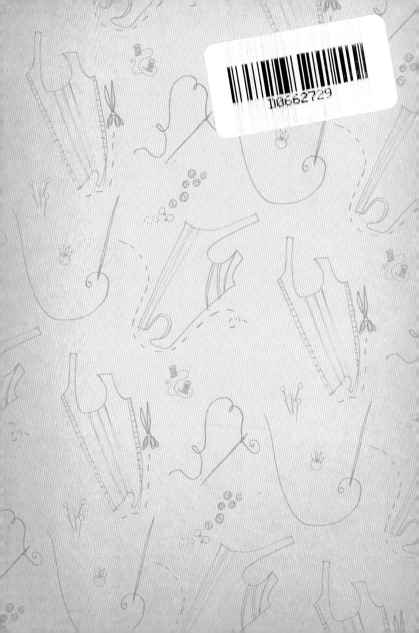

ROSE'S DRESS OF
DREAMS

ROSE'S DRESS OF
DREAMS

KATHERINE WOODFINE

with illustrations by
Kate Pankhurst

Kane Miller
A DIVISION OF EDC PUBLISHING

First American Edition 2020
Kane Miller, A Division of EDC Publishing

First published in 2018 in Great Britain by Barrington Stoke Ltd
Text © 2018 Katherine Woodfine
Illustrations © 2018 Kate Pankhurst
The moral rights of the author and illustrator have been asserted.

For information contact:
Kane Miller, A Division of EDC Publishing
P.O. Box 470663
Tulsa, OK 74147-0663
www.kanemiller.com
www.edcpub.com
www.usbornebooksandmore.com

Library of Congress Control Number: 2019940410

Manufactured by Regent Publishing Services, Hong Kong
Printed November 2019 in ShenZhen, Guangdong, China
1 2 3 4 5 6 7 8 9 10
ISBN: 978-1-68464-028-7

For Mama

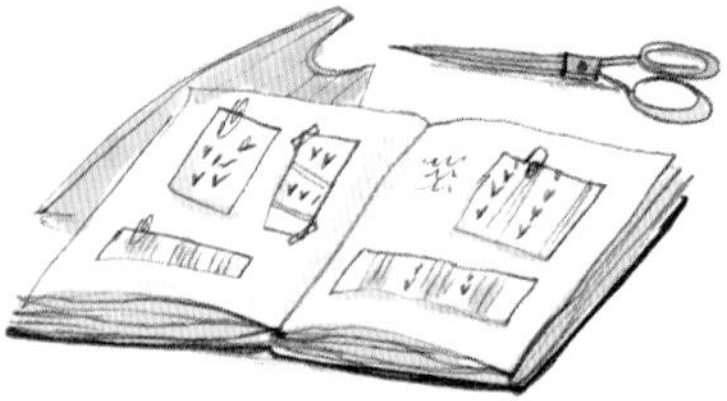

Contents

Chapter 1

Rose Dreams of Dresses

Many years ago, in the town of
Abbeville in France, there lived a girl
called Rose. More than anything else,
Rose loved beautiful dresses. She
thought about dresses when she was
supposed to be learning her lessons.
She imagined dresses when she was
supposed to be helping in the house.

Rose dreamed of dresses when she was asleep at night. Silver dresses that sparkled like moonlight. Gold dresses that glittered like treasure. Lace dresses, as delicate as the pattern of frost on the windowpane. Billowing silk dresses that swirled like the sea.

Rose dreamed of satin and velvet and taffeta. She dreamed of feathers and beads, ribbons and pearls.

Rose dreamed of dresses in a rainbow of colors. Dresses with huge skirts with ruffles and frills all over them. Dresses so beautiful that they would make anyone who wore them feel like a queen.

Each day, as Rose walked along the street in Abbeville, she watched the people go by. And Rose dreamed of how she could transform them.

She saw Josephine from the bakery, and in her daydream Rose changed Josephine's plain dress for a gown as fluffy as whipped cream.

Rose saw Suzette from the grocer's shop, and she swapped Suzette's shabby straw hat for a bonnet of juicy grapes and peaches with red cherries on top.

She saw Louise, who lived in a house with a beautiful garden, and Rose piled Louise's hair high on her head and decorated it with butterflies and roses.

She saw François, the fisherman,
and she made him a glittering jacket of
fish scales and a top hat crowned with
a ship in full sail.

Rose drew pictures of her dreams and showed them to her family. But no one seemed to understand.

"Don't be silly, Rose!" Mama said, with a frown. "Those aren't real clothes!"

"No one could ever wear a hat like that!" Papa said, with a chuckle. "They'd look ridiculous!"

As for Rose's little brother, he just pointed at her drawings and laughed.

But Rose still dreamed of dresses.

Often at night, Rose dreamed of the most beautiful dress of all. It was a dress woven out of moonlight and starlight. A dress that rippled and swished like the wind across the sea. A dress with skirts that stretched as wide as the night sky and glittered all over with stars.

Chapter 2

Rose Meets
the Fortune-Teller

One day a fortune-teller came to Abbeville. Rose made up her mind to go and see her.

Rose had no money to pay, but instead she offered the fortune-teller her own dinner. The fortune-teller ate up every scrap of the tasty meal and licked her fingers in delight. Then she told Rose's fortune.

The fortune-teller stared at the palm of Rose's hand for a long time. At last she said, "You will become a very rich woman and wear a fine dress to the Royal Court."

Rose skipped home, hungry, but very happy. One day she would go to the Royal Court and wear a wonderful dress, like the finest ladies of Paris!

But as Rose skipped along, she realized something. She didn't want to wear such a dress. What she wanted was to make one!

Rose wanted to be a dressmaker!

She imagined her busy fingers whipping up the most marvelous dresses for the ladies of the Royal Court. Dresses for duchesses and

princesses and noblewomen. Dresses
that were fit for a queen!

But there were no dresses like
those in Abbeville. If Rose was going to
be a dressmaker for the Royal Court,
she would have to go to Paris. So the
very next day Rose packed her bags,
said goodbye to Mama and Papa and
her little brother, and got on a coach
to the city.

Chapter 3

The Streets of Paris

Paris was full of crowds. Rose felt lost among all the people as she walked along the twisty gray streets.

No one was dressed in beautiful outfits. Instead their clothes were dull, and they looked poor and unhappy.

Rose walked from one dressmaker's shop to another, looking for a job. But the answer was the same everywhere.

"Non," said the first.

"Non," said the second.

"NON!" said the third.

Door after door was slammed in Rose's face.

It began to grow dark, but still Rose walked on. Soon she was very tired and cold. She wondered if she should have stayed at home in Abbeville after all. But then she came to a dressmaker's shop with windows that shone bright golden light out into the dark street.

In the window was a wonderful dress the color of emeralds and a pair of silver shoes. Rose's heart leapt.

Rose went up the steps and into the shop. She was sure they would have no job for her, but at least she could take a closer look at the beautiful emerald-green dress.

"Excuse me," Rose asked. "But might you have any work for me?"

She waited to hear "NON!" again, but instead the shop owner looked at Rose for a long time.

"Hmmmm," the owner said at last. "Well, as it happens, I have just lost my apprentice. That silly girl ran off to work for Madame Labille! So I suppose you'll have to do." The owner gave Rose a very stern look. "My name is Mademoiselle Pagelle," she said, "and I'm in charge here. You must do exactly as I say."

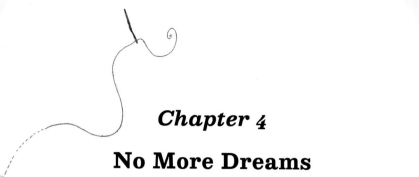

Chapter 4

No More Dreams

And so Rose started work at Mademoiselle Pagelle's shop. But she soon found out that being a dressmaker's apprentice was not at all what she expected.

Instead of designing beautiful dresses, Rose swept the floor.

Instead of sewing fabulous gowns, Rose scrubbed and polished.

Instead of trimming glorious hats, Rose ran to and fro with packets and letters for Mademoiselle Pagelle.

Rose worked so hard that when she climbed into bed at night, she hurt all over. She was far too tired to dream of any dresses — not even a single shoe!

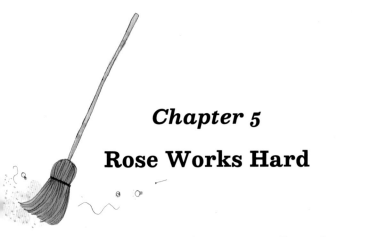

Chapter 5

Rose Works Hard

But as the winter drew near, Rose began to get used to her new life. While she swept and polished and scrubbed, she watched the dressmakers at work.

Rose began to learn about the different fabrics. She recognized the bright "shirr" sound the scissors made as they cut silk and the soft "whumph" of unfolding velvet.

Rose got to know the customers, and she listened to them as they talked about the latest fashions.

As she trudged through the snow on her errands, Rose learned to find her way around the streets of Paris. Soon, she began to dream again of dresses — and of the moonlit, starlit dress most of all.

At long last, Mademoiselle Pagelle decided that the time had come for Rose to be allowed to sew. Rose was thrilled. Was her dream of being a dressmaker at last coming true?

She took out some of her drawings to show to Mademoiselle Pagelle and the dressmakers. Rose felt sure they would all love her ideas. But instead the dressmakers began to laugh. "Hee hee hee!" they giggled.

"Oh dear," Mademoiselle Pagelle said, as she squinted and turned one of Rose's drawings upside down. "I can see you've got a lot of ideas. But these drawings are a little too ... unusual." She smiled at Rose. "Why don't you focus on helping for now?" And she gave Rose some shiny buttons to sew on a new gown.

Rose felt down at heart. She had really thought Mademoiselle Pagelle would like her ideas. Instead, she had been just like Mama and Papa. Rose started to think she might never make her fortune as a dressmaker, after all ...

But Rose still worked hard at her sewing. Even if she would never be a great dressmaker, she still loved being in the shop, surrounded by linen and taffeta, calico and silk.

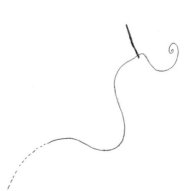

Rose soon learned all the different stitches — running stitch, backstitch, whipstitch and slip stitch. She learned to gather ruffles and make pleats and stitch a hem. She learned to piece together a skirt, and set in a sleeve, and to make a perfect buttonhole.

"Good work, Rose," Mademoiselle Pagelle said.

Chapter 6

A Dress Fit for a Princess

One day all of Mademoiselle Pagelle's dressmakers were in a fizz of excitement. They had been asked to make two new dresses for the Princesse de Conti, a lady of the Royal Court.

"We must make her dresses perfect!" the dressmakers said. "Her husband is the Prince de Conti — a very important man!"

Rose was thrilled to have the job of sewing the hems of the two gowns. She was careful to make her stitches as tiny and neat as she could.

At last, the dresses were ready. But Mademoiselle Pagelle had a terrible cold. She was shivering and sneezing. "I can't possibly deliver the dresses to the princess like this!" she wailed, as she looked at her pale face and red nose in the mirror. "But we can't keep the princess waiting. Rose, you will have to deliver the dresses instead."

Rose skipped with joy. She was going to a palace! She was going to meet a real princess!

Mademoiselle Pagelle told Rose what she must say and how she must behave in the company of such an important person.

"Don't forget to curtsey!" Mademoiselle Pagelle said. "Don't forget that you must call the princess 'Your Highness' at all times!" She was still croaking instructions as Rose set out in the coach.

Chapter 7

The Princess and the Maid

It was late and bitterly cold when Rose arrived at the palace.

She felt very small and unimportant as she made her way up to the big door, with the two precious dresses in her arms. She gave a timid knock — but there was no answer.

Rose shivered on the step. What should she do? She had to deliver the dresses. At last, she decided to open the door.

Rose stepped inside and saw a lady coming toward her. She was small and wore a plain dark dress — she must be one of the princess's maids. Rose stepped back fast, in case the maid was angry with her for being so bold as to open the door. But instead, the maid gave Rose a shy smile.

"Oh how wonderful!" the maid said. "You've come with the dresses!"

"That's right," Rose said, feeling glad. "I'm Rose. I have the new dresses to show the princess."

"Come in out of the cold," the maid said, and she took Rose into a big hall. Rose stared around at the grand room, with its glittering chandelier and elegant paintings in gold frames. The maid was welcoming and gentle, but still Rose trembled with nerves.

"Mademoiselle Pagelle has a cold, so she sent me instead," Rose said in her most polite voice. "Is the princess at home? I hope she'll like the dresses." The maid smiled at her so kindly that Rose added, "I'm sorry — I'm a bit nervous. I've never done this before!"

The maid was silent for a moment. Then she said, "I know — why don't you practice showing me the new dresses? Just while we wait for the princess? Come this way."

Rose nodded and followed the maid into a sitting room where a fire was blazing. It was wonderfully warm, and the maid poured Rose a cup of hot chocolate from a silver pot and handed her a plate of biscuits baked with spices and honey.

Rose took out the dresses, and one at a time, she showed them to the maid. Rose tried to remember every single thing that Mademoiselle Pagelle had told her to say.

The maid listened. She seemed very interested, and Rose began to enjoy herself. Soon, she forgot her nerves — and she forgot all about Mademoiselle Pagelle's instructions, too.

Instead, Rose talked about what she liked best about each dress — the swish and swirl of the skirt, the smooth feel of the satin, the rich gold trim. Before long, Rose was chattering to the maid as if they had known each other for a very long time.

Chapter 8

Rose Learns a Secret

Rose sat back in the soft chair and sipped her hot chocolate. She found herself telling the maid all about her own ideas for dresses. To Rose's surprise, the maid didn't laugh or say she was silly. Instead she just listened as Rose described all the amazing dresses she wanted to make one day.

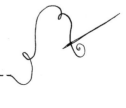

"Most of all there's one dress I dream of," Rose told the maid. "A silk dress — blue and silver like moonlight, glittering with pearls like stars." Then Rose added, "Do you know, if I made a dress for you, that's exactly the dress I would make? You'd look just like a princess!"

The maid said nothing for a moment. Then she put down her cup of hot chocolate. "I'm sorry, Rose," she said. "I've kept a secret from you. I am a princess. I'm the Princesse de Conti."

Rose jumped to her feet in horror. Mademoiselle Pagelle had given her such strict instructions about how to speak to the princess and how to behave. And now here Rose was, treating the princess's beautiful sitting room like her own home, drinking her hot chocolate and eating her biscuits — and talking as if they were friends!

Rose had mistaken the princess for a maid. She had broken all the rules. She had offended their most important customer. Mademoiselle Pagelle would never forgive her!

"Pardon me, Your Highness!" Rose began, with a curtsey. "I didn't know! I am so sorry! I beg you to forgive me for my rudeness!"

"Rose, please sit down," the princess said. "I should say sorry to you — I should have told you the truth! But when you arrived, you seemed so nervous. And I know just how that feels. I'm very shy myself, you see. I thought it would be easier for you to show me the dresses if you thought I was a maid. Besides, the truth is I don't really care about grand manners," the princess admitted. "Or the royal parties. No one ever notices me, and I feel too shy to talk to anyone. I'd much rather talk to you."

"Really?" Rose said in surprise.

"Really!" the princess said. "I've had a lovely time hearing your ideas. The moonlight dress sounds wonderful. I wish I could wear something like that!"

"But of course you could!" Rose said. "You'd look beautiful!"

"Do you really think so?" the princess asked. "I don't think I'd ever feel shy again if I wore a dress like that." She paused for a moment and then said, "These gowns from Mademoiselle Pagelle are lovely and just what I need. But I've got a very grand party soon, and I'll need another new dress for it. I've got an idea — why don't you make a dress for me, Rose? A really special dress. Will you make the dress you described for me?"

Make a dress for a princess? Rose stared at the Princesse de Conti in amazement. Of course she would!

Chapter 9

Hot Chocolate
and Honey Biscuits

For the rest of the evening, Rose and
the princess sat and talked and drank
hot chocolate and ate spiced honey
biscuits.

But at last Rose had to say goodbye. Mademoiselle Pagelle would wonder where she was. And she would have to be up early to start work on the new dress.

Rose knew just how it should be. It would be a dress to make the Princesse de Conti feel bold and brave and beautiful. Rose was already dreaming of the silk she would use, the ribbons, the pearls ...

Chapter 10

The Moon and the Stars

Back at the shop, when Rose told
Mademoiselle Pagelle and the
dressmakers the news, they couldn't
believe their ears.

"You? Make a dress for the
princess?" the dressmakers said. Again,
they all laughed.

But over the next two weeks, Rose worked very hard indeed. When she wasn't doing her work for Mademoiselle Pagelle, she drew dozens and dozens of sketches. She sewed late into the night. She cut and hemmed. She ruffled and flounced. She sewed and pleated. Rose poured everything she had learned into making the dress.

The other dressmakers soon came to help Rose when they saw how hard she was working.

Mademoiselle Pagelle gave Rose advice on her ideas and helped her to choose the right fabrics. The dressmakers showed her how to adjust the dress so it would be a perfect fit for the princess.

Rose thought about the dress all day, and dreamed about it all night.

At long last, the dress was finished.

It was a silk dress that rippled and swished like the wind on the sea. It was blue and silver like moonlight. Its skirts were as wide as the night sky, and glittered all over with pearls like stars. It had a cloak of velvet, as dark and rich as midnight, and a headdress in the shape of a silver crescent moon.

Rose gazed at the dress. It wasn't as beautiful as the dress she had dreamed of. There were so many things she wished she could do better. Rose knew she still had a lot to learn. But when the dressmakers clapped and Mademoiselle Pagelle gave her a small nod, Rose knew she had done well.

Best of all, the Princesse de Conti was delighted.

"It's wonderful!" she exclaimed, as she stroked the soft fabric. "Everyone will notice me in a dress as beautiful as this!"

Chapter 11

Dreams Come True

The Princesse de Conti wore her dress of moonlight and stars to the party.

The wide, shimmering skirts that sparkled all over with pearls filled her with confidence. The shy, quiet princess swept into the room with her head held high.

People clustered around her to admire her dress, and the princess soon forgot to feel shy as she chattered about her dress and her wonderful new dressmaker.

After the party, Rose soon had a long list of dresses to make for all the princess's new friends.

No one laughed at Rose's ideas anymore. It wasn't long before all the fashionable ladies of Paris were wearing Rose's most incredible and unusual designs. And they all wanted Rose to make them dresses to wear to the Royal Court.

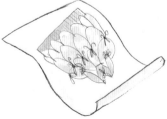

"I knew that fortune-teller had it wrong," Rose said, as she sketched one night. "My fortune was to make a dress for the Royal Court!"

Mademoiselle Pagelle was impressed. "From now on, you may consider yourself my business partner," she told Rose. "We'll run the shop together — and you can design all the dresses you want."

Rose was very happy and very excited. She had brought her dress of dreams to life, and now she could dream of all the other amazing outfits she could make. Outfits that would make anyone who wore them feel powerful and brave.

Rose dreamed of her busy fingers whipping up one marvelous outfit after another and turning the gray streets of Paris into a bright rainbow of satin and velvet, ribbon and lace.

But the Princesse de Conti was the most excited of all.

"Rose, you are going to be the most famous dressmaker in all of Paris! I just know it!" she said, as the two shared a silver pot of hot chocolate. "I think you will design dresses for the Queen of France herself one day!"

"Oh! I don't think that will ever happen," Rose said, and she laughed as she helped herself to another honey spiced biscuit. After all, dressing a real princess was quite enough to be proud of!

But a few years later, Rose would have a smart new shop of her own, and one of her best customers would be Marie Antoinette, the new Queen of France.

About the Real Rose Bertin

This story is inspired by Marie-Jeanne Rose Bertin (known as Rose), who was born in 1747.

When she was only 16, Rose traveled to Paris to become a dressmaker. After she began making dresses for the Princesse de Conti and other court ladies, her designs became very popular. She met France's

young queen, Marie Antoinette, and soon became her favorite dressmaker, creating many wonderful outfits for her.

But the people of France were poor and unhappy. They became angry with the Royal Family, and a revolution began. Soon, Marie Antoinette was arrested and sent to prison.